The Black Falcon

A tale from the <u>Decameron</u> retold by William Wise

illustrated by Gillian Barlow

Philomel Books

New York

Library of Congress Cataloging-in-Publication Data. Wise, William– The
Black Falcon: an adaptation of a tale from the *Decameron* by William Wise;
illustrated by Gillian Barlow. p. cm.   Summary: When the wealthy and now
widowed woman whom the impoverished Federigo has always loved invites
herself to his home for dinner to make a life-or-death request of him, she learns,
ironically, he has already sacrificed all he had in his love for her. ISBN 0-399-
21676-6. (1. Falcons–Fiction.) I. Boccaccio, Giovanni, 1313–1375.
Decamerone. II. Barlow, Gillian, ill. III. Title. pZ7.W778Bl 1989. (E)–dc19

First impression

For Ram and Renee,
my old and cherished friends
— W. W.

For Amy and Stella,
with love
— G. B.

A long time ago, near the city of Florence, there lived a poor young knight named Federigo Colonna. His father, a foolish nobleman, had squandered the family's vast fortune, and upon his death he had left Federigo nothing but a small country house, a few fields where a little food could be grown, and a rare black hunting hawk, called a peregrine falcon.

Federigo was extremely proud of the falcon and took it hunting almost every day. And he said to his friends, "I have neither a large house, nor a fortune in gold, nor a beautiful wife. But still, I consider myself lucky, for I possess one priceless treasure — the finest hunting hawk in all of Italy!"

Federigo lived in his country house with Emilio, his servant, an old man who had served Federigo's father for many years. Emilio prepared Federigo's simple meals, baked his bread, and took care of the house and garden. Nearby there was a great country villa, as grand as Federigo's home was modest. It belonged to a famous nobleman, the old and very rich Lord Orsini. For many years Lord Orsini and his family had been living in France, and while they were away, the villa stood empty.

Like most young knights, Federigo had been trained for only one kind of work—the work of a soldier. Except by fighting in a war, nearby or distant, he had no way of earning money, and at present there was no war in which he could bear arms. Never out of debt, he was forced to sell a few acres of land from time to time to repay his creditors, and when he did, he would console himself by remembering his one prize treasure—the rare black peregrine falcon.

One day Federigo saw a beautiful young woman riding along the road. He bowed to her and thought, "She is the loveliest woman I have ever seen. Her hair is the color of pure gold. Her eyes are a deeper blue than the summer sky. I must learn who she is and try to win her heart. For now that I've seen her, I know I shall never love anyone else as long as I live!"

When evening came, Federigo told his servant, Emilio, about the young woman. "Ah," said Emilio with a sigh, "I believe you must have seen Lady Elena. She is the wife of Lord Orsini. She and her husband and their son, Pietro, have come home to live in the great villa."

Federigo smiled to hide his bitter disappointment. "Then the old gentleman is most fortunate," he said. "He is rich, he is a man of honor, and his wife is very beautiful. Why, if he had my black falcon, he would have everything worth having in the world!"

Later when he was alone, though, Federigo no longer smiled. Morning and night, he could think of little else but his beautiful neighbor. "I would forget her if I could," he told himself. "But since I cannot, I must disguise my feelings and treat her like anyone else—with courtesy and respect, but nothing more. Because she is another man's wife, I must never show her, by a single word or deed, that I love her more dearly than life itself."

As they were close neighbors, Federigo and Lady Elena often met and exchanged a few idle remarks, but no tender words ever escaped his lips, and his severe expression never softened when he spoke to her. Lady Elena thought Federigo cold and disagreeable. "He is a man without feelings," she said to her husband. "No wonder he has never married. He cares for nothing but that peregrine falcon of his!"

But Lady Elena's son, Pietro, became fond of the poor knight, and Federigo began to feel sympathy for the boy, whose father, Lord Orsini, was too old and feeble to teach him how to hunt or fight. So Federigo, who had no son of his own, became Pietro's instructor and taught him how to draw a bow, duel with a sword, and hunt with a falcon.

Pietro often praised the knight to his mother and said that when he grew up, he wanted to be exactly like Federigo. This, however, did not please Lady Elena. "He has no heart," she said to Pietro. "Save your admiration for someone more worthy of it."

One afternoon, while jousting in a knightly tournament near Florence, Federigo was surprised to see that Lady Elena and her family were missing from their usual place in the audience. Afterward he said to one of his friends, "Where do you think Lord Orsini might be today?"

"Why, have you not heard?" his friend replied. "Last night the old gentleman's heart began to fail. The doctors could do nothing for him. It is said he died peacefully in his sleep, just before dawn."

For a full year Lady Elena dressed in black to honor her husband's memory. Federigo saw her occasionally while she was in mourning and offered his sympathy, but when he did, his expression remained cool and aloof. Though he loved her more dearly than ever, and knew that someday she might marry again, he never imagined himself a possible suitor. Lady Elena was now a very rich woman. What would she want with a poor knight such as he?

When the year was over, many great noblemen began to come to the villa to try to win the rich widow's hand. One suitor swore that he loved her because she was young and beautiful, not because she was wealthy. And yet, how tenderly his eyes seemed to linger on the gold plate and the bejeweled goblets on her banquet table. Another suitor swore that he would perish of a broken heart if she refused him. And yet, it seemed harder for him to tear his eyes away from the fine tapestries on the walls than to tear them away from her. And so, one after another, she politely thanked all of these deceitful knights and sent them away.

Lady Elena was still a young woman, though, and eventually she grew lonely. From time to time she would see her neighbor, the poor knight, out hunting or riding along the road and would gaze at his grave, handsome face, and at the falcon on his arm, and say to herself, "Ah, how that unfeeling knight loves his hunting hawk. Nothing else means anything to him. That is the way *I* wish to be loved—with all the strength and devotion which that cold-hearted man lavishes on his wretched black bird!"

During the summer Pietro fell sick with a deadly fever. The greatest doctors in Italy were summoned to the villa. They gave him potions and ordered cold cloths put on his chest and forehead. In time, the fever passed, but Pietro did not recover. Day by day he grew weaker, and as she watched him, Lady Elena began to despair. What could she do to save her child? What if she promised him a marvelous gift – something that he long had wanted – perhaps then he would take a new interest in life and begin to regain his strength.

But when she asked him if he would like a fine new horse, or a sword with a gold handle, he listlessly shook his head.

"Then tell me what you *do* want," said Lady Elena, "and I promise to move heaven and earth to get it for you."

"There's only one thing I'd truly like to have," Pietro said. "And since Federigo is my friend, if you were to ask him for it, I'm sure he would gladly give it to me."

"Ask the poor knight – for what?" said Lady Elena.

"Ask him for the black falcon," Pietro said.

Lady Elena did not know what to do. How could she ask the poor knight, who always had been so good to her son, to give up the only thing in the world he loved? And yet, if she did not ask him, Pietro might waste away and die.

Late one afternoon she sent a servant to Federigo's house with a message. "Lady Elena wishes to visit the knight on a matter of great importance. Would he receive her? Perhaps they could dine together that evening and discuss the matter then?"

The servant returned with an answer. "The knight would consider it a great honor to receive the lady."

Her message, though, had filled Federigo with dismay. Neither she nor Pietro had been inside his house before. Soon she would come there and discover just how poor he really was. His furniture was old and worn—chairs, tables, benches—and he must ask her to use them. His plate and goblets were made of common pewter, not of gold—and he must ask her to eat and drink from them. His usual supper was only a pudding, some bread, a few greens—could he ask her to suffer through such a meal?

"I will be shamed forever," he thought, "unless I can provide her with at least one dish fit to set before a queen!"

Quickly he summoned his servant, Emilio. "Lady Elena is to be my guest this evening," he said. "What do we have in the kitchen that might please her?"

"Very little, my lord," Emilio said.

"Is there venison, or some other meat, to make a stew?"

"There is no meat at all," said Emilio.

"A bit of goose, perhaps?"

"Not even the giblets, my lord."

"Well, surely you can find a chicken in the barnyard."

"The barnyard is empty," Emilio said. "Last month I killed the rooster for your supper. He was old, and if you remember, my lord, rather tough."

"Then go to the city and buy a duck or a pheasant."

"My lord, I can obtain nothing there. The merchants in Florence say they will not let me have a feather—much less a pheasant—until you have settled your debts."

Federigo sat down on one of the old chairs and put his head between his hands. "Then what am I to serve Lady Elena?" he asked in despair.

All at once the poor knight leaped to his feet, and staring like a madman, pointed to the garden. "Emilio," he cried, "I have the answer. Go outside at once and gather herbs and vegetables."

"Will you serve her a dish of vegetables, my lord?"

"Then collect firewood and prepare the stove."

"Prepare the stove for *what*, my lord?"

"For the rarest dish in all of Italy! For a dish fit to set before a queen! For the falcon, Emilio, for the black falcon! You will kill it, and pluck it, and stuff it, and roast it, and then you will set it before my guest!"

"Oh, my lord—"

Federigo frowned so darkly that his servant took a step backward, bowed fearfully, and hurried off to do as he was told. And when Federigo was alone, he said to himself, "Tonight Lady Elena shall dine on my only treasure. And when she has done so, I will be satisfied for all the days to come!"

That evening Lady Elena was too troubled herself to notice the strange smile on the knight's face as they sat down to dinner. "I eat very plainly," Federigo told her. "The bread on my table is coarse, and the pudding is simple. But I am a hunter, and sometimes I have good luck in the chase. Tonight I can offer you a small fowl that I think you will enjoy."

With great care, Federigo carved up the falcon, and Emilio placed it before Lady Elena. Then Federigo watched as the woman he loved ate all of it, wings, breast—everything. When she had finished eating the falcon, she said, "You were right, my lord, the bird was exceptional." And she smiled gently, for she had observed how little he had eaten himself—only some plain pudding and some bread—and it struck her that by coming to the poor knight's house, she might have caused him needless embarrassment and pain.

After dinner Federigo said to Lady Elena, "What is the important matter that has brought you here? For if there is any way in which I can serve you, I will do so most willingly."

"I know that it is wrong, Federigo," she said, "to ask you this favor. Pietro is very sick, though, and may not recover. I suppose he is spoiled, and that is my fault. But there is nothing except your falcon that he wants. If you could find it in your heart to be generous – to a sick child and his mother – I would count myself forever in your debt."

She watched in amazement as the poor knight's cheeks turned absolutely white. Then, without a word, he went into the kitchen, and when he returned, he held in the palm of his hand a small beak and a pair of bird's talons.

"It is too late, my lady," he said. "I no longer have a falcon to give you."

"It was the fowl that I just ate . . ."

"Yes, my lady."

"You have killed it? But why, Federigo?"

"Because I had nothing else to serve you," the poor knight said.

Lady Elena was too astonished to say anything more. She returned home, sat by Pietro's bed, and told him what Federigo had done.

"I had no idea he was so poor," she said. "I feel completely shamed. To think that for my sake—because I was his guest—he had to kill the only thing in the world that he really loved."

Before long Pietro began to recover, and eventually was able to leave his sickbed and walk around outside in the sun. At Federigo's bidding, Emilio came each morning to inquire about Pietro's health. One day Lady Elena told him that she thought his master had performed the most gallant deed she had ever known. "And yet," she said, "I still find it hard to believe that he killed his beloved falcon for the sake of a guest."

"He would have done it for no one but you, my lady," Emilio said. "He has loved you for a very long time. Ever since he first saw you—before he even knew that you were the wife of Lord Orsini."

That afternoon Lady Elena returned to the poor knight's house. She found him alone in the garden and sat down beside him. "I have talked with Emilio," she said. "And if what he says is true, when I became a widow, why did you not speak to me of your feelings?"

"I was as poor then as I am now," Federigo said.

"As poor," said Lady Elena, "and also as princely." Then she smiled, and for the first time, put her hand in his.

Lady Elena and her knight were soon married, and lived happily together with Pietro in the great villa. In time, Pietro grew up, gained his knighthood, and moved away to live on his own estate, and after that, Federigo and Lady Elena lived in the villa by themselves.

Most days their home was crowded with guests, but once each year the lady and her knight ate dinner alone.

Lady Elena served the meal herself. She put coarse bread and a plain pudding on the table. Then she brought in a small roast fowl and, carving it with great care, placed it before her husband.

"Tonight I thank you," she said, "and I do you honor. For I never shall forget that evening and the way you honored me."

And she ate only some of the bread and the pudding, while Federigo ate the roast fowl—as she once had eaten his prize black peregrine falcon.

A note about the text

The Black Falcon is an adaptation of a tale from the *Decameron*, Italian writer Giovanni Boccaccio's masterpiece written in the fourteenth century. As this is an adaptation, the story contains differences from Boccaccio's original fifth day, ninth tale, to make it suitable for use as a picture book for children. Essentially, however, the story elements are much the same as when Boccaccio first penned his great work in circa 1350. Boccaccio is generally considered the first great writer of prose in a modern language and scholars note that many writers, Chaucer and Shakespeare among them, have been greatly influenced by him. One example of this is French writer Charles Perrault's well-known "Patient Griselda" story, which is commonly credited to have its basis in Boccaccio's character Griselda from the *Decameron*.